T0096508

CLASSIC MOMENTS FROM

Romeo and Juliet

WILLIAM SHAKESPEARE

Published by Ice House Books

Copyright © 2019 Ice House Books
Illustrations by Jocelyn Kao
Original text by William Shakespeare

Ice House Books is an imprint of Half Moon Bay Limited
The Ice House, 124 Walcot Street, Bath, BA1 5BG
www.icehousebooks.co.uk

This is a celebration of the play and not intended as a direct
replica of the original text. Excerpts have been selected and some
text has been omitted to create a collection of well-loved scenes.

ISBN 978-1-912867-32-5

Printed in China

CLASSIC MOMENTS FROM

Romeo and Juliet

WILLIAM SHAKESPEARE

ICE HOUSE BOOKS

Character List

Escalus, *Prince of Verona.*
Paris, *a young nobleman and kinsman to the Prince.*
Mercutio, *kinsman to the Prince and friend to Romeo.*
Montague and **Capulet**, *heads of two houses and enemies with each other.*
Lady Montague, *wife to Montague.*
Romeo, *son of Montague.*
Benvolio, *nephew to Montague and friend to Romeo.*
Abram, *servant to Montague.*
Balthasar, *servant to Romeo.*
Lady Capulet, *wife to Capulet.*
Juliet, *daughter of Capulet.*
Tybalt, *nephew to Lady Capulet.*
Nurse *to Juliet.*
Peter, *servant to the nurse.*
Sampson and **Gregory**, *servants to Capulet.*
Friar Laurence, *a Franciscan friar.*
Friar John, *of the same order.*
Apothecary
Three Musicians
Chorus
Citizens of Verona

Scene, *during the greater part of the Play, in Verona: once, in the fifth Act, at Mantua.*

Two households, both alike in dignity,
    In fair Verona, where we lay our scene,
From ancient grudge, break to new mutiny,
    Where civil blood makes civil hands unclean,
From forth the fatal loins of these two foes

A pair of star~cross'd
lovers take their life;

Who misadventur'd piteous overthrows
    Do, with their death, bury their parents' strife.

From Act 1 Scene 2

Capulet And Montague is bound as well as I,
In penalty alike; and 'tis not hard, I think,
For men so old as we to keep the peace.

Paris Of honourable reckoning are you both;
And pity 'tis, you liv'd at odds so long.
But now, my lord, what say you to my suit?

Capulet But saying o'er what I have said before:
My child is yet a stranger in the world,
She hath not seen the change of fourteen years;
Let two more summers wither in their pride,
Ere we may think her ripe to be a bride.

Paris Younger than she are happy mothers made.

Capulet And too soon marr'd are those so early made.
The earth hath swallow'd all my hopes but she,
She is the hopeful lady of my earth:
But woo her, gentle Paris, get her heart,
My will to her consent is but a part;
An she agree, within her scope of choice
Lies my consent, and fair according voice.

From Act 1 Scene 3

Lady Cap   Marry, that marry is the very theme
I came to talk of: — Tell me, daughter Juliet,
How stands your disposition to be married?

Juliet   It is an honour that I dream not of.

Nurse   An honour! were I not thine only nurse,
I'd say, thou hadst suck'd wisdom from thy teat.

Lady Cap   Well, think of marriage now; younger than you,
Here in Verona, ladies of esteem,
Are made already mothers: by my count,
I was your mother much upon these years
That you are now a maid. Thus then, in brief; —

The valiant Paris seeks you for his love.

From Act 1 Scene 5

Romeo   What lady's that, which doth enrich the hand
             Of yonder knight?

Servant I know not, sir.

Romeo   O, she doth teach the torches to burn bright!
             Her beauty hangs upon the cheek of night
             Like a rich jewel in an Ethiop's ear:
             Beauty too rich for use, for earth too dear!
             So shows a snowy dove trooping with crows,
             As yonder lady o'er her fellows shows,
             The measure done, I'll watch her place of stand,
             And, touching hers, make happy my rude hand.
             Did my heart love till now? forswear it, sight!

For I ne'er saw true beauty till this night.

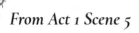

From Act 1 Scene 5

Romeo   If I profane with my unworthy hand
              This holy shrine, the gentle fine is this —
              My lips, two blushing pilgrims, ready stand

To smooth that rough touch with a tender kiss.

Juliet   Good pilgrim, you do wrong your hand too much,
              Which mannerly devotion shows in this;
              For saints have hands that pilgrims' hands do touch,
              And palm to palm is holy palmer's kiss.

Romeo   Have not saints lips, and holy palmers too?

Juliet   Ay, pilgrim, lips that they must use in prayer.

Romeo   O then, dear saint, let lips do what hands do;
              They pray, grant thou, lest faith turn to despair.

Juliet	Saints do not move, though grant for prayers' sake.
Romeo	Then move not, while my prayer's effect I take. Thus from my lips, by yours, my sin is purg'd.
	[Kissing her.]
Juliet	Then have my lips the sin that they have took.
Romeo	Sin from my lips? O trespass sweetly urg'd! Give me my sin again.
Juliet	You kiss by the book.

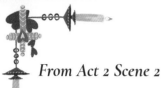

From Act 2 Scene 2

Romeo   But soft! what light through yonder window breaks?

It is the east, and Juliet is the sun! –

Arise, fair sun, and kill the envious moon,
Who is already sick and pale with grief,
That thou her maid art far more fair than she:
Be not her maid, since she is envious;
Her vestal livery is but sick and green,
And none but fools do wear it; cast it off. —
It is my lady; O, it is my love:
O, that she knew she were! —
She speaks, yet she says nothing; What of that?
Her eye discourses, I will answer it —
I am too bold, 'tis not to me she speaks:
Two of the fairest stars in all the heaven
Having some business, do entreat her eyes
To twinkle in their spheres till they return.

[...]

Juliet   Ah me!

Romeo   She speaks: —
O, speak again, bright angel! for thou art
As glorious to this night, being o'er my head,
As is a winged messenger of heaven
Unto the white-upturned wond'ring eyes
Of mortals, that fall back to gaze on him,
When he bestrides the lazy-pacing clouds,
And sails upon the bosom of the air.

Juliet

O Romeo, Romeo! wherefore art thou Romeo?

Deny thy father, and refuse thy name:
Or, if thou wilt not, be but sworn my love,
And I'll no longer be a Capulet.

Romeo   Shall I hear more, or shall I speak at this?

Juliet   'Tis but thy name, that is my enemy; —
Thou art thyself though, not a Montague.
What's Montague? it is nor hand, nor foot,
Nor arm, nor face, nor any other part
Belonging to a man. O, be some other name!
What's in a name? that which we call a rose,
By any other name would smell as sweet;
So Romeo would, were he not Romeo call'd,
Retain that dear perfection which he owes,
Without that title: — Romeo, doff thy name;
And for that name, which is no part of thee,
Take all myself.

Romeo   I take thee at thy word:
Call me but love, and I'll be new baptiz'd;
Henceforth I never will be Romeo.

Juliet   What man art thou, that, thus bescreen'd in night,
So stumblest on my counsel?

Romeo   By a name, I know not how to tell thee who I am:
My name, dear saint, is hateful to myself,
Because it is an enemy to thee;
Had I it written, I would tear the word.

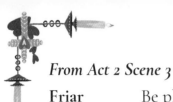

From Act 2 Scene 3

Friar   Be plain, good son, and homely in thy drift;
              Riddling confession finds but riddling shrift.

Romeo   Then plainly know,

my heart's dear love is set

              On the fair daughter of rich Capulet:
              As mine on hers, so hers is set on mine;
              And all combin'd, save what thou must combine
              By holy marriage: When, and where, and how,
              We met, we woo'd, and made exchange of vow,
              I'll tell thee as we pass; but this I pray,
              That thou consent to marry us this day.

From Act 2 Scene 5

Juliet	Here's such a coil, — come, what says Romeo?
Nurse	Have you got leave to go to shrift to-day?
Juliet	I have.
Nurse	Then hie you hence to friar Laurence's cell,

There stays a husband to make you a wife:

Now comes the wanton blood up in your cheeks,
They'll be in scarlet straight at any news.
Hie you to church; I must another way,
To fetch a ladder, by the which your love
Must climb a bird's nest soon, when it is dark.

From Act 3 Scene 1

Benvolio   Here comes the furious Tybalt back again.

Romeo   Alive! in triumph! and Mercutio slain.
Away to heaven, respective lenity,
And fire-ey'd fury be my conduct now! —
Now, Tybalt, take the villain back again,
That late thou gav'st me; for Mercutio's soul
Is but a little way above our heads,
Staying for thine to keep him company;
Either thou, or I, or both, must go with him.

Tybalt   Thou, wretched boy, that didst consort him here,
Shalt with him hence.

Romeo   This shall determine that.

[They fight. Tybalt falls.]

Benvolio   Romeo, away, be gone!
The citizens are up, and Tybalt slain:
Stand not amaz'd: —

the prince will doom
thee death.

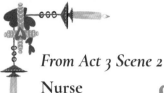

From Act 3 Scene 2

Nurse

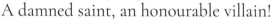
Tybalt is gone, and Romeo banished;

Romeo, that kill'd him, he is banished.

Juliet   O God! Did Romeo's hand shed Tybalt's blood?

Nurse   It did, it did; alas the day! it did.

Juliet   O serpent heart, hid with a flow'ring face!
Did ever dragon keep so fair a cave?
Beautiful tyrant! fiend angelical!
Dove-feather'd raven! wolvish-ravening lamb!
Despised substance of divinest show!
Just opposite to what thou justly seem'st,
          A damned saint, an honourable villain!

From Act 3 Scene 3

Friar   Hence from Verona art thou banished:
            Be patient, for the world is broad and wide

Romeo   There is no world without Verona walls,
            But purgatory, torture, hell itself.
            Hence-banished is banish'd from the world,
            And world's exile is death.

Friar   O deadly sin! O rude unthankfulness!
            Thy fault our law calls death; but the kind prince,
            Taking thy part, hath rush'd aside the law,
            And turn'd that black word death to banishment:
            This is dear mercy, and thou seest it not.

Romeo   'Tis torture, and not mercy:

heaven is here,

            Where Juliet lives; and every cat, and dog,
            And little mouse, every unworthy thing,
            Live here in heaven, and may look on her,
            But Romeo may not.

From Act 3 Scene 5

Lady Cap   Well, well, thou hast a careful father, Child;
One, who, to put thee from thy heaviness,
Hath sorted out a sudden day of joy,
That thou expect'st not, nor I look'd not for.

Juliet   Madam, in happy time, what day is that?

Lady Cap   Marry, my child, early next Thursday morn,
The gallant, young, and noble gentleman,
The county Paris, at St. Peter's church,
Shall happily make thee there a joyful bride.

Juliet   I wonder at this haste; that I must wed
Ere he, that should be husband, comes to woo.
I pray you, tell my lord and father, madam,

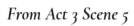

I will not marry yet;
and when I do, I swear

It shall be Romeo, whom you know I hate,
Rather than Paris.

From Act 4 Scene 1

Juliet   O, bid me leap, rather than marry Paris,
               From off the battlements of yonder tower.

Friar   Hold, then; go home, be merry, give consent
               To marry Paris: Wednesday is to-morrow;
               To-morrow night look that thou lie alone,
               Let not thy nurse lie with thee in thy chamber:
               Take thou this phial, being then in bed,
               And this distilled liquor drink thou off:
               When, presently, through all thy veins shall run
               A cold and drowsy humour, which shall seize
               Each vital spirit; for no pulse shall keep
               His natural progress, but surcease to beat:
               No warmth, no breath, shall testify thou liv'st;

The roses in thy lips
and cheeks shall fade

To paly ashes; thy eyes' windows fall,
Like death, when he shuts up the day of life;
Each part depriv'd of supple government,
Shall, stiff, and stark, and cold, appear like death:
And this borrow'd likeness of shrunk death
Thou shalt remain full two and forty hours,
And then awake as from a pleasant sleep.
Now when the bridegroom in the morning comes
To rouse thee from thy bed, there art thou dead:
Then (as the manner of our country is,)
In thy best robes uncover'd on the bier,
Thou shalt be borne to that same ancient vault,
Where all the kindred of the Capulets lie.
In the mean time, against thou shalt awake,
Shall Romeo by my letters know our drift;
And hither shall free thee from this present shame.

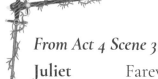

From Act 4 Scene 3

Juliet   Farewell! — God knows, when we shall meet again.
I have a faint cold fear thrills through my veins,
That almost freezes up the heat of life:
I'll call them back again to comfort me; —
Nurse! — What should she do here?
My dismal scene I needs must act alone. —
Come, phial. —
What if this mixture do not work at all?
Must I of force be married to the county? —
No, no; — this shall forbit it: lie thou there. —

[Laying down a dagger.]

How if, when I am laid into the tomb,
I wake before the time that Romeo
Come to redeem me? there's a fearful point!

Shall I not then be stifled in the vault,
To whose foul mouth no healthsome air breathes in,
And there die strangled ere my Romeo comes?
Or, if I live, is it not very like,
The horrible conceit of death and night,
Together with the terror of the place, —

[...]

O, look! methinks, I see my cousin's ghost
Seeking out Romeo, that did spit his body
Upon a rapier's point: — Stay Tybalt, stay! —

Romeo, I come!
this do I drink to thee.

From Act 4 Scene 5

Nurse   Alas! alas! — help! help! my lady's dead!
                    O, well-a-day, that ever I was born!

[Enter Lady CAPULET.]

Lady Cap   What's the matter?

Nurse   Look, look! O heavy day!

Lady Cap   O me, O me! — my child, my only life,
                    Revive, look up, or I will die with thee! —
                    Help, help! — call help.

[Enter CAPULET.]

Capulet   For shame, bring Juliet forth; her lord is come.

Nurse   She's dead, deceas'd, she's dead; alack the day!

Lady Cap   Alack the day! she's dead, she's dead, she's dead.

Capulet   Ha! let me see her: — Out, alas! she's cold:
                    Her blood is settled, and her joints stiff;
                    Life and these lips have long been separated:
                    Death lies on her, like an untimely frost
                    Upon the sweetest flower of all the field.

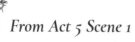

From Act 5 Scene 1

Romeo   If I may trust the flattering eye of sleep,
My dreams presage some joyful news at hand:
My bosom's lord sits lightly in his throne;
And, all this day, an unaccustom'd spirit
Lifts me above the ground with cheerful thoughts.
I dreamt, my lady came and found me dead;
(Strange dream! that gives a dead man leave to think
and breath'd such lie with kisses in my lips,
that I reviv'd, and was an emperor.
Ah me! how sweet is love itself possess'd,
When but love's shadows are so rich in joy?

[Enter BALTHASAR.]

News from Verona! — How now, Balthasar?
Dost thou not bring me letters from the friar?
How doth my lady? is my father well?
How fares Juliet? That I ask again;
For nothing can be ill, if she be well.

Balthasar Then she is well, and nothing can be ill;
Her body sleeps in Capels' monument,
And her immortal part with angels lives;
I saw her laid low in her kindred's vault,
And presently took post to tell it you:
O pardon me for bringing these ill news,
Since you did leave it for my office, sir.

Romeo Is it even so? then I defy you, stars!

Well, Juliet,
I will lie with
thee to~night.

Paris　　　This is that banish'd haughty Montague,
That murder'd my love's cousin; — with thick grief,
It is supposed the fair creature died, —
And here is come to do some villanous shame
To the dead bodies: I will apprehend him. —

[Advances.]

Stop thy unhallow'd toil, vile Montague;
Can vengeance be pursu'd further than death?
Condemned villain, I do apprehend thee:
Obey, and go with me; for thou must die.

Romeo　　　I must, indeed; and therefore came I hither. —
Good gently youth, tempt not a desperate man,
Fly hence and leave me; — think upon this gone;
Let them affright thee. — I beseech thee, youth,
Heap not another sin upon my head,
By urging me to fury: — O, be gone!

By heaven, I love thee
better than myself:

For I come hither arm'd against myself:
Stay not, begone; — live, and hereafter say —
A madman's mercy bade thee run away.

Paris   I do defy thy conjurations,
And do attach thee as a felon here.

Romeo   Wilt thou provoke me? then have at thee, boy.

[They fight.]

Page   O lord! they fight: I will go call the watch.

[Exit Page.]

Paris   O, I am slain! *[Falls.]* —
If thou be merciful,
Open the tomb, lay me with Juliet.
[Dies.]

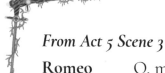

From Act 5 Scene 3

Romeo
O, my love! my wife!
Death that hath suck'd the honey of thy breath,
Hath had no power yet upon thy beauty:
Thou art not conquer'd; beauty's ensign yet
Is crimson in thy lips, and in thy cheeks,
And death's pale flag is not advanced there. —
[...]

Why art thou yet so fair? Shall I believe
That unsubstantial death is amorous;
And that the lean abhorred monster keeps
Thee here in dark to be his paramour?
For fear of that, I will still stay with thee;
And never from this palace of dim night
Depart again; here, here will I remain
With worms that are thy chambermaids; O, here
Will I set up my everlasting rest;
And shake the yoke of inauspicious stars
From this world-wearied flesh.
— Eyes look your last!

Arms, take your last embrace! and lips, O you
The doors of breath, seal with a righteous kiss
A dateless bargain to engrossing death! —
Come, bitter conduct, come, unsavoury guide!
Thou desperate pilot, now at once run on
The dashing rocks thy sea-sick weary bark!
Here's to my love! — *[Drinks.]*
O, true apothecary!
Thy drugs are quick. —

Thus with a kiss I die.

From Act 5 Scene 3

Friar   I hear some noise. — Lady, come from that nest
Of death, contagion, and unnatural sleep;
A greater Power than we can contradict
Hath thwarted our intents; come, come away.

Juliet   Go, get thee hence, for I will not away. —
What's here? a cup, clos'd in my true love's hand?
Poison, I see, hath been his timeless end: —
O churl! drink all; and leave no friendly drop,
To help me after? —

I will kiss thy lips;
Haply, some poison yet
doth hang on them,

[Kisses him.]

O happy dagger! *[Snatching Romeo's Dagger.]*
This is thy sheath; *[Stabs herself.]*
there rust, and let me die.

Friar

Romeo, there dead,
was husband to that Juliet;
And she, there dead, that
Romeo's faithful wife:

I married them; and their stolen-marriage-day
Was Tybalt's dooms-day, whose untimely death
Banish'd the new-made bridegroom from this city;
For whom, and not for Tybalt, Juliet pin'd.
You — to remove that siege of grief from her, —
Betroth'd, and would have married her perforce,
To county Paris: — Then comes she to me;
And, with wild looks, bid me devise some means
To rid her from this second marriage,
Or, in my cell there would she kill herself.
Then gave I her, so tutor'd by my art,

A sleeping potion; which so took effect
As I intended, for it wrought on her
The form of death.

[...]

At the prefixed hour of her waking,
Came I to take her from her kindred's vault;
Meaning to keep her closely at my cell,
Till I conveniently could send to Romeo:
But, when I came, (some minute ere the time
Of her awakening,) here untimely lay
The noble Paris, and true Romeo, dead.
She wakes; and I entreated her come forth,
And bear this work of heaven with patience:
But then a noise did scare me from the tomb;
And she, too desperate, would not go with me,
But (as it seems,) did violence on herself.

From Act 5 Scene 3

Prince   Where be these enemies? Capulet! Montague! —
            See, what a scourge is laid upon your hate,
            That heaven finds means to kill your joys with love

Capulet   O, Brother Montague, give me thy hand:
            This is my daughter's jointure, for no more
            Can I demand.

Montague   But I can give thee more:
            For I will raise her statue in pure gold;
            That, while Verona by that name is known,
            There shall no figure at such rate be set,
            As that of true and faithful Juliet.

Capulet   As rich shall Romeo by his lady lie;
            Poor sacrifices of our enmity!

Prince   For never was a story of more woe,

Than this of Juliet and her Romeo.